# blue aliens!

## An Adventure in Color

Written by Tony Porto

Conceived and designed by 3CD

Tony Porto, Mitch Rice, and Glenn Deutsch

 LITTLE, BROWN AND COMPANY

New York ⌁ An AOL Time Warner Company

For our moms and dads — who protected us from space aliens, monsters, and lots of other scary stuff

Last night I watched this

REAL SCARY MOVIE on TV.

In it, a whole bunch of GREEN space aliens landed on Earth and started gobbling up everything that was GREEN.

They feasted on **GREEN** grass, bushes, and trees,

Green grass can grow very tall. The tallest kind is bamboo. It can grow as high as 120 feet!

and snacked on GREEN bugs

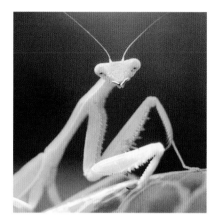

and lizards by the tons —
just like they were eating french fries.

The green bug up at the top is a praying mantis. It's the only insect that can turn its head from side to side.
This green lizard is a chameleon. He can change colors. Let's hope he wasn't green when the aliens came.

Gangs of **GREEN** aliens chewed **GREEN** eyeballs,

Human **eyes**, whether they are **green** or not, have more than 2 million working parts.
This eye has no working parts. It's a fake.

tennis balls, and olives.

(They spit out the yucky red stuff in the middle.
Who could blame 'em?)

In the official rules of tennis, only white or yellow balls are allowed. Green tennis balls are not.
Some trees that grow green olives are over 2,000 years old!

They had just polished off GREEN Bay and were headed to South America to munch an entire rain forest...

Although rain forests cover only a small part of Earth, they contain more than one half of all the kinds of green plants and animals found in the whole world.

when into our TV room stormed the

# SCARIEST ALIEN I had ever seen.

It screamed in a scratchy alien voice—

# GOTOBEDTHISMINUTE!

# IT'SASCHOOLNIGHT!

# YOUCAN'TWATCHTHIS!

# YOU'RETOOYOUNG!

# GETTOBEDNOW!

In the glowing **BLUE** light of the TV,

The first **televisions** didn't glow **blue** at night because their pictures were only in black and white. Since TVs were invented, more than one billion sets in black and white and in color have been sold!

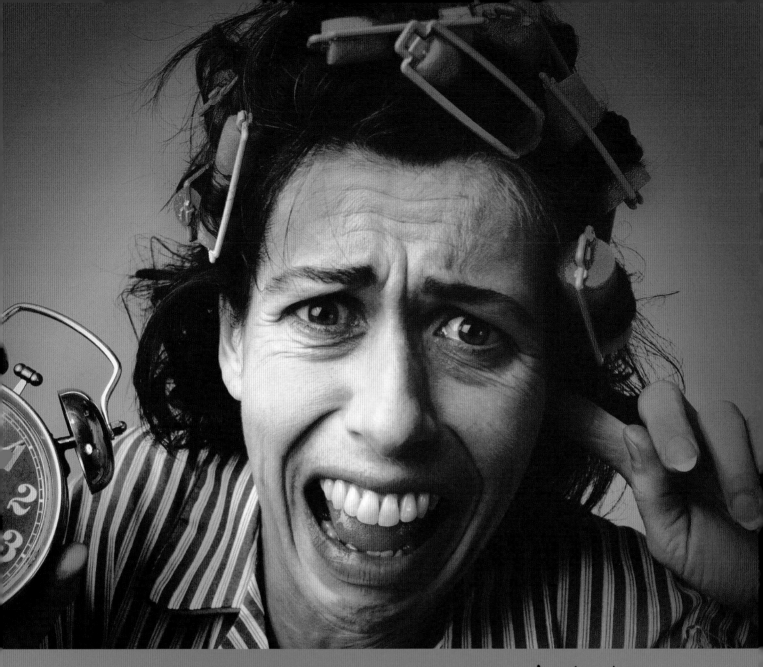

Mom sure looked like a horrible alien. And when any alien speaks, especially the mom kind, I LISTEN.

So I ran as quick as I could up to bed, buried my face in my pillow, and tried my hardest to forget aliens of EVERY kind.

This morning, things got WORSE...

# MUCH WORSE.

To begin with, my all-time favorite BLUE jeans that I wear to school nearly every day were missing. I searched the piles of clothes on my bedroom floor, and even the kinda STINKY heap hidden under my bed, but there wasn't a trace of them.

It was almost as if they had run away!

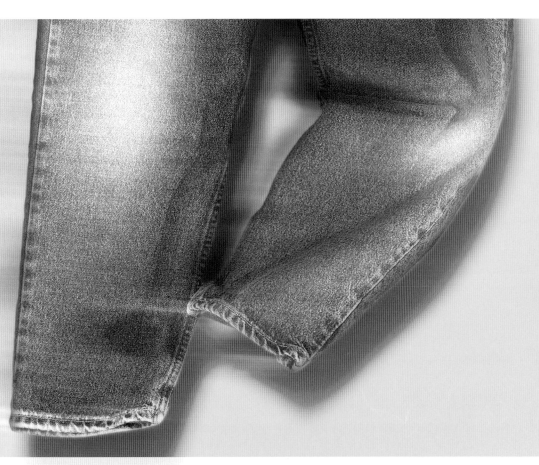

The oldest pair of **blue jeans** in the world were found in an empty California silver mine (and not in a stinky clothes pile under a bed). They were made around 1890.

At breakfast, my BLUEberry toaster waffle had ONE puny BLUEberry in the whole thing!

Dad said it was what you call a "fluke"— ya know, a goofy thing that happens once in a BLUE moon.

At one time blueberries were called star berries. Can you see why?
Every once in a great while the moon appears blue in color. That's why "once in a blue moon" means a rare event.

Well, when my "fluke" popped out of the toaster, that one puny BLUEberry was gone! Dad said it must have been loose and fallen into the toaster, and that that was sort of a fluke, too.

As I was trying to decide which was worse, my missing BLUEberries or Dad yacking on about flukes, THE SCARIEST, MOST AWFUL IDEA HIT ME FROM OUT OF THE BLUE.

The old expression "from out of the blue" means from out of the sky—some place unknown.

Last night's movie was right.
Aliens ARE eating stuff on Earth!

But that stuff
ISN'T GREEN—
IT'S BLUE!

Through the rest of the day I saw more and more proof of hungry **BLUE ALIENS.**

On my walk to school, alien-controlled clouds were chomping up huge chunks of **BLUE** sky by the minute.

The sun gives off light in all colors of the rainbow, but the sky looks blue because blue light gets scattered around more than most other colors.

Water in lakes and oceans is supposed to be BLUE—right? Well, the stuff I slurped at the drinking fountain before class was CLEAR.

Somehow they sucked out the BLUE!

Whether it's blue or not, Americans use as much as 700 billion gallons of water each day.

The **BLUE** whales we studied during Mrs. Sapphire's morning science lesson weren't really **BLUE**. They were gray!

That's right, **BLUE** whales are gray! And no one seemed to notice or care—not even Mrs. S.

Blue whales are the largest whales and the largest animals ever to live on Earth—even larger than dinosaurs! By the way, whale tails are called "flukes" (though they look nothing like toaster waffles).

In Arts class, we listened to a kind
of sad music that Mrs. S just "loves."
It's called THE BLUES.

In one song,
a singer howls out
that he is "BLUE."

He **MUST** be an alien!

Use of the word **"blues"** to mean sadness can be traced back to England in the 1500s.
**Blues music** grew out of the sadness felt by African-American slaves. This guy is **blues** great BB King.

At lunch, the cafeteria served Meatloaf Surprise. The only real surprise was that the glob of meat on my tray looked as **BLUE** as it always does.

I guess even **BLUE** aliens won't eat some things.

It's believed that the first **cafeteria** opened in Kansas City, Missouri, in 1891. It probably served **blue** Meatloaf Surprise, too!

But by far, the **WORST** disaster of the day came during our afternoon spelling test.

First, the aliens ate every piece of my **BLUE**-lined paper, and that's the only kind we are allowed to use for tests!

If one ton of blue-lined paper gets recycled, it saves about 17 trees.

Then, I tried asking my friend Perry for some, but as he turned around to talk to me, Mrs. Sapphire screeched at him—

"FACE FORWARD, MR. WINKLE!"

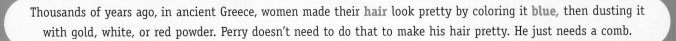
Thousands of years ago, in ancient Greece, women made their **hair** look pretty by coloring it **blue,** then dusting it with gold, white, or red powder. Perry doesn't need to do that to make his hair pretty. He just needs a comb.

The only choice I had was to use leftover paper from one of my old reports.

I didn't think Mrs. Sapphire would be happy about this. And I knew for SURE that she wasn't when she asked to see me after class.

When the bell rang, Mrs. S said good-bye to the class from her desk. She seemed busy licking star stickers and putting them on **EVERYONE ELSE'S** spelling papers.

Like **star** stickers, stars in the sky come in lots of colors. **Blue** stars are very large. When they die, the light they give off can be brighter than an entire galaxy.

I tried my best to be calm as I came up to her, but just as she was about to lick a BLUE star, everything that was on my mind came gushing out.

# BLUE ALIENS ATE MY BLUE-LINED PAPER!

They've been chomping, munching, and slurping all kinds of BLUE stuff— sky, whales, jeans, and BLUEberries!

AND THAT'S JUST FOR STARTERS!

for a second, Mrs. Sapphire smiled.
(Really, that's her smile.)

Then she said that the reason she wanted to see me was because I did poorly on my test, and she didn't care AT ALL about the type of paper I used.

She told me to concentrate and not let my "overactive imagination get the best of me."

She also said that BLUE aliens are NOT eating stuff because

"THERE ARE NO SUCH THINGS AS ALIENS."

I feel a whole lot better now that
I talked with Mrs. S.

I'm gonna try to **STOP** my imagination
from being "overactive," too. Just as soon
as I figure out one teeny, tiny thing.

As I thanked Mrs. Sapphire and started
to walk away, I'm not sure if she licked that
**BLUE** star she'd been holding in her hand, or if she...

# SWALLOWED IT!

I think I'll have to keep my eye on her.

Thanks to our wives and kids: Mary, Anne, John, Laura, Max, Adam, Laura, Owen, Seth, and Calvin (Glenn's newest little guy).

Special thanks to our friend Marko Neely for his superb photoshop illustrations, and to these friends, too: Marcia Biasiello, Big D, Kevin Brown, Jeffrey Bower, Dan Casadas, Mysti Cobb, Gary Gifford, Sean Hare, Amy Hsu, Nikki Limper, Will and Teddy Marszalek, Maria Modugno, Chuck Quinn, Charlie Seymour, and Howard Yaffe.

These are more folks who helped us with **Blue Aliens!**: Corbis, Photodisc, Stone, and Taxi.

The authors' photograph is by Sharon Hoogstraten Photography.

First Edition

Library of Congress Cataloging-in-Publication Data

Porto, Tony.
    Blue Aliens! : an adventure in color / written by Tony Porto ; conceived and designed by 3CD, Tony Porto, Mitch Rice, Glenn Deutsch. — 1st ed.
        p. cm.
    Summary: After staying up late to watch a scary movie, a boy awakens to find that blue things are missing, from his favorite jeans to his blue-lined notebook paper, and he is certain that aliens are the reason.
        ISBN 0-316-61359-2
    [1. Blue—Fiction. 2. Extraterrestrial beings—Fiction. 3. Schools—Fiction.] I. Rice, Mitch. II. Deutsch, Glenn. III. Three Communication Design. IV. Title.

PZ7.P8377 Bl 2003
[E]—dc21                                                                                        2002192458


10 9 8 7 6 5 4 3 2 1

SCPCO

Manufactured in China

The text for this book is set in 3CD Kid Font (created by Tony Klassen) and Officina Serif.

a blue strea

blue in

blue

blue blood

from out o

once in a

blue suede

blue jay li